Samuel French Acting Edition

Wolf at the Door

by Marisela Treviño Orta

‖SAMUEL FRENCH‖

be invented, including mechanical, electronic, photocopying, recording, videotaping, or otherwise, without the prior written permission of the publisher. No one shall upload this title(s), or part of this title(s), to any social media websites.

For all enquiries regarding motion picture, television, and other media rights, please contact Concord Theatricals Corp.

MUSIC USE NOTE

Licensees are solely responsible for obtaining formal written permission from copyright owners to use copyrighted music in the performance of this play and are strongly cautioned to do so. If no such permission is obtained by the licensee, then the licensee must use only original music that the licensee owns and controls. Licensees are solely responsible and liable for all music clearances and shall indemnify the copyright owners of the play(s) and their licensing agent, Concord Theatricals Corp., against any costs, expenses, losses and liabilities arising from the use of music by licensees. Please contact the appropriate music licensing authority in your territory for the rights to any incidental music.

IMPORTANT BILLING AND CREDIT REQUIREMENTS

If you have obtained performance rights to this title, please refer to your licensing agreement for important billing and credit requirements.

WOLF AT THE DOOR was first produced by the New Jersery Repertory Company (Suzanne Barabas, Artistic Director; Gabor Barabas, Executive Producer) in Long Branch, New Jersey on October 18, 2018. The performance was directed by Daniel Jáquez, with sets by Jessica Parks, lights by Jill Nagle, sound by Merek Royce Press, and costumes by Patricia E. Doherty. The production stage manager was Rose Riccardi. The cast was as follows:

ISADORA . . . . Desiree Pinol
YOLOT . . . . Alexandra Lemus
ROCÍO . . . . Liz Zazzi
SÉPTIMO . . . . Oscar A. L. Cabrera

WOLF AT THE DOOR then received a National New Play Network Rolling World Premiere at participating theaters: Kitchen Dog Theater (Dallas, Texas), Milagro (Portland, Oregon), and Halcyon Theatre (Chicago, Illinois).

CHARACTERS

ISADORA – A wife. Barely 20.

YOLOT – The interloper. In her 20s.

ROCÍO – A servant. In her 50s or 60s. Isadora's childhood nurse and nanny, now her housekeeper.

SÉPTIMO – A husband. In his 30s. Uncommonly handsome and charming.

SETTING

Mexico. A *hacienda* far from anything.

TIME

Once upon a time. Winter.

AUTHOR'S NOTES

NOTE ON CASTING

Ages of characters do not have to be strictly adhered to when casting roles. Feel free to cast actors who embody the sense of youth or age needed for each role.

NOTE TO THE DIRECTOR

A word of caution. I urge you to resist being too precious with the poetic language in this play. To do so is a trap. It weighs down the language and has a soporific effect on the audience. Instead, let the delivery be pedestrian – ordinary speech. The poetry will lift itself up on its own.

NOTE ON SOUND

Wolf howls should increase in volume over the course of the play to indicate they are encroaching on the *hacienda*.

NOTE ON LINE CHANGES

These lines [*] and stage directions can be dropped or altered depending on production needs. For example, if Yolot is not chained to the bed, but rather the fire place, then the line can be altered to "chained up." Also "what is that?"

SPANISH WORDS AND PHRASES

¿a dónde vas?: where are you going?
abre la puerta: open the door
amor mio: my love (term of endearment)
atole: hot beverage, thickened with masa and flavored with cinnamon and brown sugar
buenos dias: good morning
buenas noches: good evening
cabrón: bastard
criada: servant
deme un leño: give me a piece of firewood
¿de qué hablas?: what are you talking about?
desgraciado: (calling someone a) disgrace
despiértate: wake up
es un demonio: he's a demon
hacienda: ranch
hasta la muerte: until death
hermanos: brothers
hija: daughter (can be used as a term of endearment)
¡jodida!: fucked
la familia: the family
lo veo: I see it
madre de Dios: mother of God
madre purísima: holy mother (Virgin Mother)
¿me entiendes?: do you understand me?
mentirosa: liar
mi bisabuela: my great-grandmother
mi familia: my family
mi'jita: my daughter (contraction of mi hija – my daughter)
mi'jito: my son (contraction of mi hijo – my son)
Mictlán: Aztec land of the dead
mujer: woman
no, para nada: no, not at all
no sé: I don't know
no te preocupes: don't worry
para servirle: at your service
pero: but
que bueno: that's good
que descanses: sleep well
¿qué te dije?: what did I tell you?
querida: dearest (term of endearment)
regalo de Isis: gift of Isis
señor: sir, mister
sí: yes
¡suéltala!: let her go

te (lo) juro: I swear
traiganos algo para comer: bring us something to eat
tu marido: your husband
valeriana: valerian, a root used to make a tea with soporific effects
¡ven pa'ca, mujer!: come here, woman
vete, vieja: get going, old woman
vieja: old woman
¿y, por qué?: and why? (for what reason)

PRELUDE TO *WOLF AT THE DOOR*

A scratch at the door. It isn't that animal of a husband, or one of the wolves that have descended on your *hacienda*, it's something more primal. A drive. A will to live, survive and protect your young. Tonight you'll have the upper hand and the good sense to know when to open and when to lock that door.

Scene One

(The front room of an 1840s hacienda, a fire in the hearth and near the fireplace a bed, obviously out of place. Light from the setting winter sun filters through a window near the bed. Offstage a woman moans. Enter **ISADORA** *in a nightgown. She is pregnant and has a black eye – almost faded. She holds her pregnant belly with one hand and grabs onto furniture, the wall, to steady herself.)*

ISADORA. Rocío!

*(**ISADORA** continues toward the bed.)*

Rocío!

*(Enter **ROCÍO** carrying towels and a cup of tea.)*

ROCÍO. *¿Qué te dije?* You were supposed to stay in bed.

ISADORA. You said walking around would help the baby come faster.

ROCÍO. Never mind what I said. Here, drink this.

ISADORA. What is it?

ROCÍO. *Valeriana.* It will help you sleep when it's over.

*(**ISADORA** drinks the tea.)*

Come on now. Into bed.

*(**ISADORA** does not get into bed, but continues to walk around the room.)*

Walking around to make the baby come faster – this baby is coming early as it is. Four weeks early, *hija.*

ISADORA. He's impatient. I can feel his feet pressing against my ribs. I think he's going to come sprinting into this world.

ROCÍO. That's good. He'll need speed to outrun Séptimo. He's the kind of man who might eat his own young.

ISADORA. Not now, *vieja*.

(A painful contraction hits **ISADORA**.*)*

ROCÍO. Why not now? It's his fault you're early. What did he think would happen? Throwing you against a wall, *Madre de Dios*. He's insane. In your condition. In any condition. *Es un demonio*.

ISADORA. *(Resigned.)* And he's my husband.

ROCÍO. That's no excuse. *¿Y, por qué?* What have you ever done to deserve the back of his hand?

ISADORA. I can't move fast enough anymore. It's like I'm made of honey. And that only makes him angrier.

He broke another cup. He grabs them too tightly. The porcelain cracks like eggshell. The coffee scalds his hand. And every time he blames the cup.

He's the predictable one, you just have to get out of the way. Like a storm on the horizon.

*(***ISADORA*** cries out as she experiences a strong contraction.)*

Tell me, *vieja*. Will it hurt?

*(***ROCÍO*** gently touches* **ISADORA***'s black eye.)*

ROCÍO. No more than your life does already.

ISADORA. *Mi familia* arrives in less than a month. That means no more black eyes. No more bruises. At least until they're gone. And this. It will heal up. Just in time for our visitors.

ROCÍO. If your brothers knew what that *cabrón's* done to you, they'd string him up the nearest tree.

ISADORA. Séptimo wouldn't go down without a fight. He'd take a few of them with him.

And besides, he's a man with powerful friends.

ROCÍO. Your father's friends are just as powerful.

ISADORA. No. Father's friends are honorable men. But Séptimo's…any of my brothers who did survive would find themselves in front of a firing squad or worse. There's no getting out of it, *vieja*. I am Séptimo's wife. *Hasta la muerte.*

> *(In the distance a wolf howls.* **ISADORA** *notices.)*

ROCÍO. ...When *la familia* leaves, we could go with them.

ISADORA. But not with his child. He wouldn't stand for that. And I'm not abandoning my baby.
Accept it. We're left to fend for ourselves.

ROCÍO. That we could do without him just fine.

ISADORA. *(Urgent.)* Rocío. What if he heard you?

ROCÍO. He'd turn me out with only the clothes on my back. But not to worry. He's out riding that horse of his. He treats that animal better than you I think.

ISADORA. No. Even his love has a kind of burden to it.

> *(***ISADORA*** *experiences a contraction.)*

It hurts!

> *(***ROCÍO*** *helps* **ISADORA** *get into bed and opens her legs for delivery.)*

ROCÍO. Of course, it does. The power to give life is a great gift. Did you think something that miraculous could fit between your legs? It's like the finger of God pressing open a door inside you. To give life you have to give up a little of your own, that's what's breaking inside of you, *hija.*
Now, push.

> *(***ISADORA*** *pushes.)*

I remember when you were born, *mi'jita.* Your mother was so desperate for a daughter. Six children. All boys.
She would only let your father touch her during a full moon. They say the moon, in her glory, brings you daughters. Almost drove your father crazy. Now there's a man who knows how to love a woman.

> *(***ISADORA*** *pushes.)*

Right before you were born I found your mother outside in the middle of the night. She said she was looking for the new moon. I think she was hoping to find luck in it. Nine months pregnant in just her nightgown. But her belly was the only white orb to be found that night.

> (**ISADORA** *pushes.*)

I had to remind her that the new moon is invisible. It joins that part of the world unseen by human eyes. But even though it's beyond our sight, its power touches everything.

You were born right as dawn began to break. You were her miracle. Finally, a daughter.

> (**ISADORA** *gives one final push and the baby is finally delivered. Both women let out gasps of relief.*)

(Beaming.) A son!

> (**ISADORA** *reaches for her baby. It takes a moment before both* **ISADORA** *and* **ROCÍO** *realize the baby is not crying.* **ROCÍO** *begins to urgently massage its chest and lightly pat its back.*)

ISADORA. No, no, no...

> *(The unimaginable horror takes hold of* **ISADORA.***)*

> *(Eventually,* **ROCÍO** *stops trying to revive the baby. She looks at* **ISADORA** *and shakes her head.* **ISADORA** *cries.)*

> *(Solemnly and slowly* **ROCÍO** *swaddles the baby and rises from the bed. Eventually* **ROCÍO** *begins to move toward a door leading to the rest of the house.)*

(Urgent.) Wait.

> (**ISADORA** *extends her arms to receive the baby. With tender ceremony* **ROCÍO** *places*

the baby in the cradle of **ISADORA**'s *arms.* **ISADORA** *looks at her baby and cries quietly.)*

(A moment passes. The front door of the house flies opens. **SÉPTIMO** *enters, the door slams behind him. He carries animal traps, chains. He goes to the window and looks out.)*

SÉPTIMO. They're avoiding the traps.

There's a pack of wolves up on that hill. Sitting. Watching the house. Stare at them long enough and you can almost see them thinking. Calculating.

I put the dogs in the stable. When wolves are hungry enough they'll send down a bitch in heat to lure a dog away. Before he knows what's happening, they're tearing the flesh right off his bones.

*(***SÉPTIMO*** finally notices the state of his wife, the silent baby. He goes over to* **ISADORA**, *lifts the blanket to inspect the baby's face, and drops the blanket.)*

(Coldly.) What happened?

ROCÍO. *(Under her breath.) Desgraciado.*

(To **SÉPTIMO***.)* Out. Get out!

SÉPTIMO. This is my house, *vieja.*

ROCÍO. You want to know what happened? You want to know who to blame? You did this. You!

What are you going to tell *la familia* when they arrive? What will you say became of their grandson?

SÉPTIMO. *(Restrained flicker of humanity.)* A son?

ROCÍO. *Sí.* Your <u>dead</u> son.

SÉPTIMO. A son...

(To **ISADORA***.)* At least you got that right.

*(***SÉPTIMO*** goes to the door. Opens it and pauses.)*

(Matter-of-factly.) Bury it.

(**SÉPTIMO** *exits with the traps and chains.* **ROCÍO** *embraces* **ISADORA** *so that the baby is held by* **ISADORA** *and* **ISADORA** *is held by* **ROCÍO.**)

ROCÍO. Sleep, *hija.* Sleep. Close your eyes and let this world slip away. And pray. Pray to forget the anguish of this life: the bruises, the empty cradle of your arms. Dream it all away. Dream through this winter.

(**ISADORA**'s *eyes are closed.* **ROCÍO** *lays* **ISADORA** *to sleep.* **ROCÍO** *then takes the baby and exits out the front door of the* hacienda.)

(*Lights shift.*)

Scene Two

*(In the dark, the mournful howl of a wolf. Lights up on **ROCÍO** outside near the stable, snow on the ground. Behind her is the door to the stables. As she speaks, **ROCÍO** uses a shovel to dig a small grave. She then carefully arranges the swaddled stillborn baby into a small wooden crate that's filled with hay.)*

ROCÍO. You have her face. The same sweet nose. Perhaps it is better this way, *mi'jito*. Better that you not see her like this, the way she tries to hide the pain, the sorrow – how she limps through this life. Better that you never know him. He would have polluted you.

There. You almost look like you're sleeping. I'm putting you next to the stables, near our dogs. They will keep you company.

When I was a little girl, *mi bisabuela* used to say that dogs carry the spirits of the dead across a deep river to the afterlife. She told us that it was how you died that determined your fate. Determined which paradise your spirit went to.

Warriors who died in battle, mothers who died in childbirth – they went to their own paradise. Those who died ordinary deaths had to make a long, hard journey through Mictlán. They would have to face challenges and tests before their souls would be purified. Before they could find rest.

But little ones like you, they went to a paradise where milk dripped from the tree branches. And there they waited for a second chance at life.

How I wish I could give you that second chance.

*(**ROCÍO** puts the lid on the crate and puts it into the grave. She places stones on top of the crate and buries it.)*

I pray this is the only time I have to do this, *mi'jito*. Take my prayers with you. You'll be so much closer to God. Maybe He will hear you.

(The sound of excited, happy barking. **ROCÍO** *opens the stable door and sleeping in the hay amongst the dogs is* **YOLOT**, *naked and pregnant.)*

Madre purísima.

*(***ROCÍO*** crosses herself.* **YOLOT** *awakens and quickly covers her belly as if to protect it.)*

No te preocupes. No one's going to hurt you.
Who did this to you?

YOLOT. No one did anything to me. I was tired and your dogs invited me to share the straw.

ROCÍO. Here put this on before you catch your death.

*(***ROCÍO*** grabs a horse blanket or serape and puts it on* **YOLOT**.*)*

YOLOT. Usually it's Death that does the catching, *vieja.*

ROCÍO. But where on earth did you come from? The nearest *hacienda* is days away and here you are without clothes, without a horse.

YOLOT. I came across the river last night.

*(***YOLOT*** yawns, stretches, there is something almost dog-like in how she relishes these gestures.)*

ROCÍO. You waded through freezing water?

YOLOT. There's a log spanning the distance between the two banks. We crossed it.

ROCÍO. "We"?

YOLOT. My brothers and I. They're still out there, waiting for me.

ROCÍO. Where?

*(***ROCÍO*** goes to the stable door and looks out.)*

YOLOT. Up on the hill.

ROCÍO. I don't see anyone.
Wait.

(The howl of a wolf.)

They're watching the house. Just like he said.

YOLOT. They're hungry. Like me.

ROCÍO. If you wait here I can bring you something. I'd invite you in, but –

YOLOT. You don't have to explain. I can smell it from here. And on your hands.

> *(**YOLOT** takes **ROCÍO**'s hands and brings the tops of them to her nose.)*

Wood. Hay. Freshly dug earth.

You washed him before burial.

And...something else. Something wild. Untamed. Almost...dangerous.

ROCÍO. ...What are you?

YOLOT. A porter. I am a beast of burden. Mine is the most precious cargo.

> *(**YOLOT** caresses her belly. A wolf howls.)*

It's time for me to go.

> *(**ROCÍO** helps **YOLOT** to her feet.)*

Tell me your name.

ROCÍO. Rocío.

YOLOT. I will remember your kindness.

> *(**YOLOT** takes **ROCÍO**'s hands. This time she inspects her palms.)*

There's blood on your hands.

ROCÍO. *¿De qué hablas?* They're clean.

YOLOT. Are they?

> *(**ROCÍO** quickly pulls her hands away and unconsciously wipes them on her clothing. **YOLOT** approaches and peers into **ROCÍO**'s eyes, examining her soul.)*

Here it is. You turned a blind eye. You held your tongue. And she suffers for it.

ROCÍO. *(Astonished.)* ...I – I know what you are.

> (**SÉPTIMO** *enters and watches the women.*)

YOLOT. Then you know it's time for me to go. Here, I won't be needing this.

> (**YOLOT** *almost removes the shawl she's wearing but stops when* **SÉPTIMO** *speaks.*)

SÉPTIMO. *Buenas noches.*

> (**ROCÍO** *steps in front of* **YOLOT** *as if to protect her.* **YOLOT** *is curious about their interaction.*)

ROCÍO. She was just leaving.

SÉPTIMO. *(Feigned concern.)* Leaving? In her condition? No, I don't think so. Especially not in the dead of night. In the middle of winter.
What kind of family would we be if we didn't offer her shelter? Or something to eat?
Are you hungry? Rocío roasted a chicken for supper. The bird cooked in its own juices for hours until the meat just fell right off the bone. Made me want to lick my fingers down to the marrow it was so good.
Would you like some?

> (**YOLOT** *is salivating.* **SÉPTIMO** *is now very close to the women.*)

YOLOT. ...Chicken?

SÉPTIMO. Rocío, why don't you go to the house. Prepare a plate for our guest.

ROCÍO. I think you ate it all, *Señor.*

SÉPTIMO. No, Rocío. There was plenty of meat still on that carcass. Why don't you go fetch some of that chicken?

> (**SÉPTIMO** *takes one step towards* **ROCÍO** *to make his point. She backs away and begins to leave the stable.*)
>
> (**ROCÍO** *rushes into the next scene.*)
>
> (*Lights shift.*)

Scene Three

(**ROCÍO** *rushes into the house and tries to awaken* **ISADORA**.)

ROCÍO. *(Urgently.)* Isadora, *despiértate*. Wake up, *hija*.

(**ISADORA** *turns her back to the audience and remains in bed, asleep.*)

You have to wake up now. *Tu marido*, he's –

(*Enter* **SÉPTIMO** *dragging a struggling* **YOLOT** *by the nape of her neck – the horse blanket has been fashioned into a sort of makeshift poncho that she wears.* **SÉPTIMO** *has attached some sort of leash to her neck, a metal collar attached to a chain. He secures the chain around the metal frame of the bed, locks it.* **YOLOT** *tries to bite at him, it's as if being held by the nape of her neck hits a very raw nerve, but she is no match for his strength. All the while the wolves outside are howling, a sort of nervous and distressed cacophony.*)

(**SÉPTIMO** *releases* **YOLOT** *from his grasp and steps just out of her reach. She lunges at him ready to claw his eyes out.* **SÉPTIMO** *laughs.* **YOLOT** *tries to remove her collar.*)

YOLOT. Take this <u>thing</u> off me.

SÉPTIMO. No.

(*Beat of intense animosity.*)

You're a fighter. That's good. It means your baby will be strong. Will survive.

(**SÉPTIMO** *notices* **ROCÍO**.)

Didn't I tell you to get our guest something to eat?

(**ROCÍO** *exits to the kitchen.* **SÉPTIMO** *takes a chair and straddles it.* **YOLOT** *takes in her surroundings.*)

(Businesslike.) Believe it or not Fortune is smiling on you. On both of us. Fortuitous. That's the word for it. You see we each need something the other has.

I've seen women like you before. Women whose honor has been...compromised. Turned out of their homes by their fathers. No protectors. Nowhere to go. No means to survive.

I can change that.

I can relieve you of the one burden you are unprepared to care for. The one thing that will stand in the way of any kind of respectable marriage or future.

And if you play your cards right, you'll leave here better off than you came.

Compensated.

And all you have to do is one little thing. A trade.

> *(With his hand, **SÉPTIMO** reaches out and references the shape of **YOLOT**'s pregnant belly.)*

> *(**YOLOT** immediately covers her belly.)*

YOLOT. This isn't for you.

SÉPTIMO. I disagree.

> *(Beat.)*

> *(**ROCÍO** enters with a plate of cold chicken. She offers it to **YOLOT**. **YOLOT** continues her face off with **SÉPTIMO**. Finally, unsure what to do, **ROCÍO** puts the plate of food onto the floor.)*

In a little less than a month my wife's family will arrive. They're coming to celebrate the first year of our marriage. And on this anniversary, they're expecting to see our firstborn. And by the looks of you, that baby will be coming along any day now.

Vete, vieja. It's time to retire.

> *(**SÉPTIMO** rises from his chair and ushers **ROCÍO** out of the room.)*

(To **YOLOT**.*) Que descanses.*

> *(***YOLOT** *watches them exit, listens intently to see if they'll return. The only noise is the crackling of the fire in the hearth and the occasional wolf howl.)*
>
> *(After a while,* **YOLOT** *begins to quietly pull at the chain attached to her leash, every so often looking to see if* **SÉPTIMO** *will return. She pulls at her collar, again at the chain, puts her feet against the bed and pushes. Gradually her efforts make more noise and she jostles the bed.* **ISADORA** *awakens, she does not immediately see* **YOLOT**.*)*

ISADORA. I had the strangest dream.

> *(***ISADORA** *looks down at her body, touches her empty belly.)*

I had...

> *(She shuts her eyes and takes her hand off her empty belly.)*

No... No. This is a bad dream. When I wake up it'll be like every morning since you first fluttered inside me. My back will ache as I pull myself out of bed and you'll be kicking your little feet so hard...
I just have to wake up.
Wake. Up.

> *(***YOLOT** *moves and* **ISADORA** *hears the chains rattle.* **ISADORA** *opens her eyes.)*

(Startled.) Who's there? Rocío?

> *(***YOLOT** *doesn't respond. Cautiously* **ISADORA** *moves toward the end of the bed to see who's there.* **YOLOT** *crouches.*)*

It's no use. I can see you.*

> *(Slowly* **YOLOT** *sits up.)*

Are you a part of my dream?

YOLOT. No. But we share the same nightmare.

ISADORA. Do you know what happens next?

YOLOT. More of the same.

> (**YOLOT** *moves, her chain rattles.*)

ISADORA. What was that?*

YOLOT. I'm chained to the bed...like you.*

ISADORA. I'm not chained.

YOLOT. Yours are the worst kind.

> (**YOLOT** *pulls at her collar.* **ISADORA** *moves closer.*)

ISADORA. Who put that on you?

YOLOT. You know who.

ISADORA. There's no escaping him, is there? Even in sleep.

YOLOT. You have to try harder.

ISADORA. Is that what you did?

YOLOT. I was distracted.

> (**YOLOT** *remembers the chicken. She takes the bowl of chicken and eats.* **ISADORA** *watches her.*)

ISADORA. I wonder what Rocío will say when I tell her about this dream. She'll probably say you're an omen. Another sign that we should leave this place before we can't.

YOLOT. She would have a point.

> (**YOLOT** *puts down the bowl of bones and is once again irritated by her collar. She pulls at it.* **ISADORA** *moves close and tries to touch the collar.*)

ISADORA. May I?

> (**YOLOT** *pulls away – unsure, cagey.*)

It's all right. I won't hurt you.

> (**ISADORA** *shows* **YOLOT** *both her hands.* **YOLOT** *smells them and then allows* **ISADORA** *to inspect the collar.*)

It's no use. You'll need a key.

YOLOT. My brother once caught his foot in a pair of iron
teeth. He gnawed his way free.

ISADORA. Through the iron?

YOLOT. ...No.

> (*Beat as* **ISADORA** *understands.*)

> (*The wolves begin to howl urgently. They
> sound a little closer than before.* **YOLOT** *jumps
> up to the window, leans against it.*)

(*Urgent.*) Listen. They're worried about me.

I had to come down alone. Because of the dogs. So they
stayed on the hill. Too far away to help.

> (**YOLOT** *notices* **ISADORA** *staring at her
> pregnant belly. She puts her hands over
> herself protectively.*)

You. You were the mother.

I can smell the grief coming off your skin.

ISADORA. (*In denial.*) Don't say that.

YOLOT. Why not?

ISADORA. Because this is my dream and I decide what
happens in it.

YOLOT. You're a strange creature.

ISADORA. I could say the same about you.

YOLOT. What's your name?

ISADORA. Isadora.

YOLOT. Isadora. That's a powerful name. *Regalo de Isis*, the
goddess who brought back the dead.

ISADORA. And you? What is your name?

YOLOT. Yolot. In my tongue it means "heart."

ISADORA. What "tongue"?

YOLOT. Nahuatl. It used to be the language of an empire.
But now so many of the old ways are disappearing.
Except for me and my brothers.

> (*A mournful wolf howl.*)

ISADORA. It sounds so sad...heartbroken.

(**YOLOT** *dries the tears in her eyes.*)

YOLOT. He is.

(**YOLOT** *pulls at her collar and chain.*)

(*Urgent.*) I have to get this thing off me. I have to get back. I'm not meant to stay here on this side –

(**YOLOT** *experiences a small contraction.* **ISADORA** *tries to get out of bed to help* **YOLOT**, *but experiences pain – she looks back down at her empty belly then at* **YOLOT**.)

ISADORA. This isn't a dream, is it?
It happened, didn't it?

YOLOT. Yes.

ISADORA. ...Am I awake now?

YOLOT. Almost.

(**YOLOT** *walks away from the window.*)

ISADORA. Please. You need to rest.

(**YOLOT** *cautiously sits on the foot of the bed.*)

You don't have to sleep at my feet.

YOLOT. I prefer it here.

(*The women sit facing one another, mirroring each other.*)

ISADORA. Do you know how long? ...Until it happens?

YOLOT. A day. Maybe two. The younger ones are always eager for this world. They feel cheated.

ISADORA. The "younger ones"? I don't understand.

YOLOT. That's all right.

ISADORA. (*With difficulty.*) ...What do you think the baby is? ...A boy or a girl?

YOLOT. A boy.

ISADORA. (*With strained emotion.*) I had wanted a girl. A girl I could have kept safe. He wouldn't have been interested in a daughter.

YOLOT. But it was a boy.

ISADORA. Yes. A beautiful little boy. But he wouldn't have stayed that way. If I hadn't lost him tonight I would have lost him eventually. Séptimo would have molded him in his own image. He would have become like his father.

YOLOT. Vicious.

ISADORA. He wasn't always this way.

YOLOT. *(Intrigued.)* He...changed?

ISADORA. Yes... No, that's a lie. That's what he was. A lie dressed up. He hid what he really was, from all of us.
If I had known I never would have... And my family never would have consented.

  (Beat.)

I was the youngest. The only daughter of a wealthy landowner.
And there were suitors. Many suitors. All of them eager for my dowry.
It was easy enough to see through them to their true purpose. But my family was patient. I was allowed to send them all away with their tails between their legs.
But Séptimo. He didn't come as a suitor. He was a friend of my brothers. A man's man, they told me.
So they thought.
Unlike my suitors, he never really spoke to me. In fact, he avoided me. If I came into the room he would stop whatever he was doing. He never said, *"Buenos días,"* or "Good afternoon." All he'd ever say was my name.
"Isadora."
The way he said it. You'd think he was seeing the Pacific for the first time. Or naming some undiscovered country. As if saying my name took the very breath out of him.
On my nineteenth birthday, when other men brought me flowers he brought me a stone. A large oval stone from a riverbed. And then he finally spoke to me. Really spoke to me.

He said the rock was smooth because of all the time the river had flowed over it. That the water had polished the stone, removed all of its rough edges. He told me to touch it. To feel it. Its sleek surface. That I was touching the passage of Time.

My mother thought it was a strange gift. A rock. But I ran my hands over it every night. Its hard, smooth surface. I closed my eyes and imagined I was placing my hand on his chest. That I could feel the passage of Time in his skin.

A few weeks later he came to buy one of my father's mares. I hid in the stables and watched him with the animal. Watched how he spoke softly into its ear, gently brushed the length of its body.

How little I knew about the art of deception.

A month later we were married. Two days after the ceremony we moved here.

YOLOT. And the mare?

ISADORA. She hates him. But she's too afraid to try and throw him. 'Cause if the fall doesn't break his back, he'll break hers.

(A wolf howls in the distance.)

Sleep. You'll need your strength for tomorrow.

YOLOT. I have enough to spare for the both of us.

(Beat. The women settle down to sleep.)

ISADORA. Yolot, what does grief smell like?

YOLOT. Like mother's milk, but stale.

Goodnight, Isadora.

(Lights dim. The wolves howl mournfully.)

Scene Four

*(The howling of wolves in the night from the previous scene gives way to dawn as sunlight comes through the window. **ISADORA** awakens and sees **YOLOT**. She then looks down at her empty belly. Eventually, **ISADORA** carefully gets up and goes to open the door to the kitchen.)*

ISADORA. *(A loud whisper.)* Rocío. Rocío.

*(**ISADORA** returns to the bed and adjusts the covers over **YOLOT** who remains deep in sleep.)*

I wanted you to be a dream. But you really are here and my baby...my son...is gone.

*(Enter **ROCÍO**.)*

ROCÍO. Isadora, you should be in bed.

ISADORA. There's already someone in it.

ROCÍO. Yes, all sorts of strange happenings this morning. The chickens won't eat. And the milk's gone sour.

ISADORA. Where is Séptimo?

ROCÍO. *No sé.* I haven't seen him.

ISADORA. I need to speak with him.

ROCÍO. First, let's put some proper clothes on you. And find some for her.

*(**ISADORA** and **ROCÍO** exit. A moment later **SÉPTIMO** enters through the front door. Loudly he throws another log on the fire and stokes the embers. The noise of this awakens **YOLOT**.)*

*(As **SÉPTIMO** speaks it's as if he's a different person, he seems kind, concerned.)*

SÉPTIMO. *Buenos días.*

> *(No reply from **YOLOT**.)*

Did you sleep well?

> *(**SÉPTIMO** waits for a reply from **YOLOT**. She gives no response.)*

I – I know it's not ideal sharing a bed, but it's close to the fire at least.

We brought the bed in here for my wife, Isadora. Lately the nights have been too brutal for her.

> *(Another awkward silence.)*

What's your name?

I understand. Last night I was rather forceful.

I'm not the sort of man who forces a woman to stay when she wants to go, but I ask you to see it from my point of view. A woman – naked and pregnant – out in the bitter, winter cold. Determined to expose herself and her unborn child to the elements. Without food. Without clothes. Wandering around in the dead of night.

And when I put my hands on you – you went wild. Uncontrollable. A danger to yourself. To the baby.

What was I to do? I had to bring you inside. Had to make sure you wouldn't run off. So I apologize if I was a bit rough with you. That wasn't my intention. Truly.

> *(**YOLOT** seems to relax a bit, but is still weary of **SÉPTIMO**.)*

Are you hungry?

> *(**SÉPTIMO** exits to the kitchen. A moment later he returns with a bowl.)*

Here you are. Rocío makes excellent *atole*. Nice and hot.

> *(Slowly and carefully he puts the bowl in front of a still, watching **YOLOT**. When he moves away she picks up the bowl and eats.)*

That's good. You'll need your strength.

> *(He straddles the chair again and watches her eat.)*

I – I didn't introduce myself last night. Séptimo Chavez, *para servirle.*

And by now you've probably met my wife Isadora. She hasn't been herself lately. Last night we...last night we lost our son.

<u>My</u> son.

> **(SÉPTIMO** *suppresses his grief.* **YOLOT** *stops eating and closely watches/listens to* **SÉPTIMO.***)*

I've been waiting all my life to start a family. I never really had one, you see. That legacy was denied me.

My in-laws, they're expecting a grandson. Instead they'll find a grave.

If I could, I'd put myself in it. Anything to bring back my son. I was going to give him everything I never had. He was going to be *my new beginning.*

Of course, Isadora and I can have more children, but this first child was important. Firsts are significant. They set the tone for everything that follows. I mean, how does it look? And appearances are important. Very important. They instill confidence. Trust.

(Careful.) That's why I suggested an...understanding. Between us. I can help you. If you help me.

Have you thought about my offer?

(Pleading.) Entrust your child to my care. I will take good care of him, *te juro.* The best. And you will be generously cared for.

If you agree.

> *(No response from* **YOLOT.***)*

> **(SÉPTIMO** *is beginning to lose patience.)*

I know you can speak. You talked enough last night.

> **(SÉPTIMO** *waits.* **YOLOT** *stares silently at him.)*

(Pressing.) Say something.

> (**SÉPTIMO** *rises from the chair and walks away from* **YOLOT**. *He stands by the window staring out. A change comes over him – his body, his voice.)*

(Aggressive.) You don't want to talk? Fine. Then you'll listen. I can talk enough for the both of us.

I'm used to the silent treatment. Grew up with it. Same with beatings. I was fair game for my brothers. And my father. He never intervened. He told me it would make a man out of me. It did. It taught me the one lesson this world has to teach: that only the strong survive. That the weak are ground underfoot. And every day you have to exert your force, your will on others in order to maintain your foothold and the moment you don't the walls close in and you'll be nothing but a stain on them.

> (*With his thumb,* **SÉPTIMO** *gestures a digging out motion with the next line.)*

After my brother Porfirio lost an eye my brothers finally left me alone.

But not my father. He never failed to remind me that I was nothing more than an unwanted son. Told me I'd never make anything of myself. That as soon as I came of age I was on my own.

And I was. Out on my own at fifteen. A feral boy.

But I coped. I learned how to blend in. How to be exactly what everyone wanted to see.

And I swore I would raise myself up. I would show my brothers and my father exactly what kind of man they had turned their backs on. And everyone – everyone – would see that I am what my father failed to be: a successful family man.

And here I am. A man of property. Married into a good family. A wealthy family. A family that <u>expects</u> a grandson. And I intend to give it to them. So when they look at me all they'll see is a strong, capable man. That's all they ever need to see.

I meant what I said. That child isn't only for them. It's for me. I intend to give my son all I was denied growing up. The life. The inheritance. Everything.

> *(Beat.)*

Do you believe in Fate? I do. How else can you explain a pregnant woman who appears on my property just as my own son is lowered into his grave.

You're here for a reason.

YOLOT. It's not what you think.

SÉPTIMO. Isn't it? I know you. You're feral. We can smell our own kind.

Did you run away? Did they take everything away from you, even the clothes off your back?

I'm not a man who takes "no" for an answer. And if I have to, I'll rip it right out from between your legs.

But I'm sure it won't come to that.

You're going to accept my offer. I'm going to compensate you for your trouble, but make no mistake that child is staying here...and you won't be. *¿Me entiendes?*

YOLOT. I understand you. Better than you think. But you do not have my consent.

SÉPTIMO. *(Amused.) Mujer,* I don't need it.

YOLOT. That's where you're wrong. On both counts.

> *(Enter* **ISADORA** *and* **ROCÍO** *carrying clothes for* **YOLOT.***)*

SÉPTIMO. *Buenos días, amor mio.* I'm sure by now you've become acquainted with our guest. She'll be staying with us until the baby is born. And then she'll be leaving. Leaving this house. Leaving our land. Leaving her child.

ISADORA. *(Tentative.)* Séptimo...unchain her.

SÉPTIMO. No. You can't let a wild animal run free, *querida.* I'm keeping her here for her own good.

ISADORA. You can't take the baby.

SÉPTIMO. Don't tell me what I can and cannot do.

Don't worry, Isadora. I will take good care of our guest. She'll leave here much better off than how we found her. And the baby will be better off, there's no doubt about that.

(**SÉPTIMO** *takes* **YOLOT***'s chin in his hand.*)

I once saw a cat eat her entire litter. There's no telling what this one will do.

(**YOLOT** *bites his hand fiercely.* **SÉPTIMO** *cries out in pain and immediately moves to strike her, but* **ISADORA** *gets in his way.*)

ISADORA. *(Firmly.)* Remember what happened the last time you struck a pregnant woman.

(**SÉPTIMO** *grabs* **ISADORA***'s face, looms over her ready to strike.*)

SÉPTIMO. And you? You're no longer with child.

ISADORA. Careful where your hand lands, Séptimo. Fresh bruises won't heal until <u>after</u> my family arrives.

(**SÉPTIMO** *releases* **ISADORA***. He pulls out a handkerchief and wraps his injured hand.*)

SÉPTIMO. You'll find I can be a patient man. We'll finish this after the baby comes and after your family leaves.

(**SÉPTIMO** *exits.* **YOLOT** *spits in his direction after he's gone.*)

YOLOT. He tastes foul.
(To **ISADORA***.)* Thank you.

ISADORA. You're welcome.

(**ISADORA** *sees the empty bowl of atole. She hands it to* **ROCÍO***.*)

Rocío, *traíganos algo para comer.*

ROCÍO. I made biscuits. *Pero*, they didn't rise.

ISADORA. That's fine.

(**ROCÍO** *hands the clothes to* **ISADORA** *and exits.* **ISADORA** *begins to dress* **YOLOT** *in a nightgown.* **YOLOT** *lets her.*)

(After a beat **YOLOT** *speaks.)*

YOLOT. You stood up to him.

ISADORA. Yes.

YOLOT. You've never done that before.
You surprised him. Made him nervous.

ISADORA. I don't think anything can make that man nervous.

YOLOT. You did. Made something inside him pause. He may be good at hiding his true self, but I saw it. Saw it spasm.

> *(***ISADORA*** *takes a brush to* **YOLOT***'s hair.* **YOLOT** *pulls away.)*

ISADORA. It's only a brush... For your hair.

> *(***ISADORA*** *begins to carefully brush* **YOLOT***'s hair. She pulls it back and secures it with a barrette.)*

YOLOT. You're different this morning.

ISADORA. Am I?

YOLOT. Yes. Don't you sense it?

ISADORA. ...I do.
Rocío was right. Childbirth breaks something inside of you. A shell cracks open and falls away. It's where we keep that part of ourselves we're taught to hide.

YOLOT. The price of domestication.

ISADORA. *(Amused.)* I suppose that must be it. From an early age, I was taught to be obedient. To honor my mother and my father. That I should do the same for a husband.

YOLOT. Even a husband like him?

ISADORA. They never told me about husbands like him. I didn't know they existed.

YOLOT. There's a lot they didn't tell you.

ISADORA. Yes, there's a lot I had to learn on my own. How far away to stand to be out of reach. How long a black eye takes to heal. How to make myself small and unseen.

YOLOT. That doesn't sound like you.

ISADORA. *(Matter-of-factly.)* But it is.

YOLOT. No. You stopped his hand. You stepped into harm's way to shield me. That took strength. Courage.

ISADORA. I don't know where it came from.

YOLOT. Perhaps your hidden self is emerging.

ISADORA. And what hides inside me?

YOLOT. The ferocity of an animal protecting its young.

ISADORA. ...I have no young.

YOLOT. No. But something has been unleashed. An instinct all its own.

ISADORA. When I was a girl I raised a brood of chicks. Watched each one hatch so that I was the first creature they saw. They thought I was their mother. They used to follow after me instinctively. Maybe it works the other way around as well. A mother without a child and the first new creature I see...is you.

I won't let him harm you, *te lo juro.*

YOLOT. I know.

> (**ROCÍO** *returns with food for* **YOLOT***: a cold, flat biscuit. As* **YOLOT** *begins to eat* **ISADORA** *grabs a shawl and puts it on.)*

ROCÍO. *¿A dónde vas?*

ISADORA. To find Séptimo. I need to talk to him.

ROCÍO. Do you think that will work?

ISADORA. I have to try, *vieja* – for her.

ROCÍO. He won't give up what he wants that easily.

ISADORA. No, he won't.

ROCÍO. Then what makes you think you can change his mind?

ISADORA. Because this time there's something that I want.

> (**ISADORA** *exits through the front door.)*

> (*Lights shift.)*

Scene Five

(Lights up on **SÉPTIMO** *in the stable. The sound of the mare, unseen, snorting and moving around in her stall.* **SÉPTIMO** *hangs his saddle over the side of the stall, prepping it for a ride.)*

*(***ISADORA** *enters tentatively, standing near the entrance of the stable. At first,* **SÉPTIMO** *doesn't look at her when he speaks.)*

SÉPTIMO. We've done this before, haven't we?
 The first time you watched me in a stable you hid and I pretended not to know you were there. So much depended on what you saw. What you thought you saw...of me.
 That moment. Your heart. My whole future.
 What do you see now, Isadora?

ISADORA. I see a man in pain.

SÉPTIMO. What do you know about pain? You grew up with a family that loved you. That wanted you.
 You wouldn't understand.

ISADORA. You're wrong. I'm the one person who knows you better than anyone else. Haven't we lived under the same roof for almost a year now? I know your moods. Know your face. Every so often I see the man my brothers brought into my parents' home.

SÉPTIMO. *(Scoffing.)* Still that naïve and sheltered girl. Seeing what you want to see.
 That man I pretended to be – it was a ruse.

ISADORA. How can anyone "pretend" to be good without knowing something about goodness? Even the smallest seed can become a tree.

SÉPTIMO. Is man a tree? No. He's an animal. Like those wolves out there. And an animal is what it is. You can't change it.

ISADORA. Tell that to a caterpillar in its cocoon.

(Tentative.) That man you pretended to be…that man I fell in love with…he could be real, if you wanted him to be.

We could have a new beginning, you and I.

> *(The phrase "new beginning" catches his ear. He thinks for a moment.)*

SÉPTIMO. …And what becomes of the last year?

ISADORA. We put it behind us. Like a bad dream, we awaken from it.

SÉPTIMO. You make it sound easy. Like closing a door and opening another.

ISADORA. We can do it together. But you have to let me in. You asked me what I see.

SÉPTIMO. "A man in pain."

ISADORA. I see more than that. I see the man who told me about riverbeds and currents. I see –

SÉPTIMO. *(Matter-of-fact.)* Subterfuge.

> **(ISADORA** *takes this in.)*

ISADORA. *(Eventually.)* Did you ever love me?

SÉPTIMO. Love is a fevered dream. A bedtime story.

I'm sure you've heard many. All with a happily ever after. Want to know the story I was told growing up?

Once upon a time there was a man and a woman who were madly in love. They had six sons. And the husband was so proud he spoiled each and every one of them. He thought he had the perfect family. But his wife, his wife longed for the one thing he hadn't given her: a daughter. So when she became pregnant for the seventh time the wife was happy.

Too happy.

You wouldn't think a man could be jealous of his unborn child. But he was. And a darkness crept into his heart. Into his home.

One moonless night the child was born. But it wasn't a girl. And the birth was difficult.

Too difficult.

And as her son took his first breath she exhaled her last.

Another son. An unnecessary son.

They hated him. His brothers. Not just because they adored their mother, but because they remembered what their father had been like before. What their lives had been before.

Before I was born.

They wanted nothing to do with me. They cast me out. I have no family except the one I make for myself. And my son...my son was supposed to change everything. He was supposed to be my new beginning, my legacy.

(**SÉPTIMO** *punches the side of the stall. The horse snorts in agitation.* **SÉPTIMO** *punches the side of the stall again and again – working himself into a sob that takes over his whole body. The horse responds with neighs and squeals matching the intensity of* **SÉPTIMO**'s *punching and settles down as he stops.)*

(**ISADORA** *carefully approaches and reaches out to him, a comforting hand on his back.)*

ISADORA. You do have family, Séptimo. You have me.

(**SÉPTIMO** *looks at* **ISADORA** *as if for the first time – really seeing her. He kisses her passionately, forcefully.* **ISADORA** *is caught off-guard. She lets him kiss her, but she does not kiss back – the kiss is off balance and we can see she is not reciprocating, but letting herself be kissed.)*

SÉPTIMO. Did you really mean it? That we could put the past behind us?

ISADORA. Yes. We can write our own ending. Happily ever after.

(**SÉPTIMO** *buries his head in* **ISADORA**'s *bosom.)*

ISADORA. We'll start again. From scratch. Build ourselves from the ground up. And that man you pretended to be – you can be reborn in his image.

(*Beat as she comforts him.*)

But every new journey has a first step. A step toward that new beginning. A step you must take.

Séptimo... I need the key to unlock Yolot's collar.

(*A change passes over* **SÉPTIMO**.)

She can't be kept here against her will. We have to set her free.

SÉPTIMO. You want the key? That's what this is all about, isn't it?

(**SÉPTIMO** *grabs* **ISADORA** *by the nape of her neck viciously. He removes the key ring from his belt and holds them up high and jingles them.*)

(*Mocking.*) "It's going to be all right. A new beginning, you and I!"

ISADORA. I meant it!

SÉPTIMO. *¡Mentirosa!*

(**SÉPTIMO** *releases her and reattaches the key ring to his belt.*)

ISADORA. I wasn't lying!

Séptimo, listen to me. We can tell them...my family... about our baby.

SÉPTIMO. And what exactly would you tell them?

ISADORA. I can make them understand.

SÉPTIMO. (*Agitated.*) Understand what? That my seed is weak. Or that you are? They'll want to know where to lay the blame. I won't have anyone meddling in my private affairs.

ISADORA. They're my affairs, too.

SÉPTIMO. Listen to you. So spoiled. So coddled. You have no idea how the world works. Your family made you weak, Isadora. You don't have the will to do what needs to be done. And this needs to be done. We will have a baby when your family arrives.

ISADORA. No.

SÉPTIMO. No?

ISADORA. No. No, I won't let you take her baby. Things are going to change around here, Séptimo.

SÉPTIMO. Are they? And why would they?

ISADORA. Because if I have to, I'll tell my brothers –

(SÉPTIMO grabs ISADORA by the throat. The unseen horse snorts and moves in agitation.)

SÉPTIMO. Listen to me, Isadora. And listen well. Nothing, NOTHING, is going to change around here. And if you think I'll let your brothers drive me off of my land, then you're sorely mistaken. Because I have a long-range rifle I'm testing out this afternoon on the wolves. And I'm sure I have enough bullets for them and every single one of your brothers. I'll pick them off one by one as they ride up to the house. You can count on it.

(SÉPTIMO releases ISADORA. SÉPTIMO takes his saddle and enters the stall to put it on his unseen horse.)

It should have been you who died.

(SÉPTIMO exits. The sound of the mare snorting.)

(Offstage.) (To mare.) Easy. Easy.

(The sound of SÉPTIMO exiting the stable, making clicking sounds to urge his horse along.)

(ISADORA waits until he's gone and then looks at the tools hanging on the stable wall behind her. She picks up a hammer and examines it.)

(Lights shift.)

Scene Six

(Lights up in the hacienda *front room.* **YOLOT** *stands at the window looking out.)*

YOLOT. He's going somewhere.

*(***ROCÍO*** *joins* **YOLOT** *at the window.)*

ROCÍO. Where is she?

YOLOT. Still in the stable.

ROCÍO. Maybe I should check on her.

YOLOT. No.

She's all right.

*(***YOLOT*** *experiences a labor contraction. Her contractions are quickly followed by the sound of the wolves howling – louder, closer.)*

They know something's wrong.

ROCÍO. You should rest. You'll need your strength.

*(***ROCÍO*** *helps* **YOLOT** *into bed.)*

YOLOT. I've never kept them waiting before.

ROCÍO. Are they...like you?

YOLOT. Not completely. They do not change form. It is not their purpose. They are here only to escort me back, to keep me safe.

I'm vulnerable like this. In this body. But your kind comes into the world and leaves it the same way.

ROCÍO. Defenseless.

YOLOT. Yes.

My brothers and I, we're interlopers in this world. That makes us subject to its natural laws. The longer we stay the more risk.

*(***YOLOT*** *touches her belly.)*

I can feel him moving. And each kick has more and more substance.

ROCÍO. ...She doesn't know what you are. Or what you're carrying.

YOLOT. She doesn't need to know.

ROCÍO. I don't like keeping secrets from her.

YOLOT. *(Without judgment.)* But you've done it before, haven't you?

(**ROCÍO** *is taken aback.*)

ROCÍO. Only once have I kept the truth from her.

YOLOT. *(Without judgment.)* Once was damage enough.

ROCÍO. Don't you dare lecture me.
Do you think I don't know? Each bruise, each black eye – I feel it. A hundred times right here.

(**ROCÍO** *presses against her breast.*)

It's my fault. And I'll do penance every day of my life.

YOLOT. And probably some afterward.

ROCÍO. *Sí.* And probably some afterward.

(*Enter* **ISADORA.**)

ISADORA. Quick. We don't have much time.

ROCÍO. Where is he?

ISADORA. Checking on the traps he's laid.

YOLOT. *(Renewed urgency.)* I have to warn them.

(*In the distance the report of a rifle causes the women to freeze.*)

ISADORA. *(To* **ROCÍO.***)* Can you see anything, *vieja?*

ROCÍO. *No, para nada.*

ISADORA. Good.

(**ISADORA** *reveals her hammer and approaches* **YOLOT.***)*

Here. Let's try with this.

Rocío, *deme un leño.*

(**YOLOT** *joins* **ISADORA** *on the floor in front of the hearth.* **ROCÍO** *brings a piece of firewood to* **ISADORA,** *puts it on the floor and holds it steady.*)

Hold the chain tight.

> (**YOLOT** *and* **ROCÍO** *hold the chain tight over the firewood.* **ISADORA** *strikes it. After the third strike,* **ISADORA** *pauses.*)

ROCÍO. *(Urgent.)* Don't stop.

> (**ISADORA** *strikes the chain three more times.*)

ISADORA. *(Deflated.)* It's not working. We've only flattened it a little.

YOLOT. Try one more time.
Please.

> (**ISADORA** *strikes the chain again three more times. A metallic snap.*)

> (**YOLOT** *scurries away from the bed dragging a bit of chain along the floor with her.* **YOLOT** *remembers the metal collar and pulls at it.*)

ISADORA. You can take that off later. I'll give you the tools to take with you.

YOLOT. Can't you take it off now?

ISADORA. There's not enough time. You need to put as much distance between you and Séptimo as possible. *(To* **ROCÍO**.*)* Quick, go get something to keep her warm and some food.

YOLOT. No. I don't need any of that.

ISADORA. But the cold.

YOLOT. I'll be fine.

ROCÍO. Listen to her, *hija.*

ISADORA. All right. But then at least take one of the horses. You'll need to be fast if you want to outpace Séptimo.

> (**ISADORA** *helps* **YOLOT** *to her feet.* **YOLOT** *experiences a contraction and cries out.*)

Are you all right?

YOLOT. Yes, but we have to hurry. There isn't much time.

ISADORA. If the baby is coming you have to stay.

YOLOT. No. I must leave.

ISADORA. You can't have this baby alone in the woods.

YOLOT. I can't have it yet. I have to get back across the river. Please. I will be all right.

(Reluctantly **ISADORA** *helps* **YOLOT** *walk to the door.)*

ISADORA. Rocío, *abre la puerta.*

*(***ROCÍO** *opens the door to reveal* **SÉPTIMO** *with the carcass of a wolf draped over his shoulders. The women recoil. He throws the dead wolf onto the floor.* **YOLOT** *screams at the sight of it and goes to the animal's lifeless body, crying.* **SÉPTIMO** *quickly grabs* **YOLOT** *by the nape of the neck. She fights with a mixture of mourning, hatred and labor pains.* **SÉPTIMO** *forces her to look at the dead wolf.)*

SÉPTIMO. You like that? I think I'll make a little fur coat out of it...for the baby.

*(***ROCÍO** *tries to help* **YOLOT**.*)*

ROCÍO. *¡Suéltala!*

*(***SÉPTIMO** *throws* **ROCÍO** *into a wall. She sinks, dazed.)*

ISADORA. Let her go!

*(***ISADORA** *rushes* **SÉPTIMO** *and slaps him. Hard.* **SÉPTIMO** *freezes.* **ISADORA** *returns his glare.)*

SÉPTIMO. That's it, *mujer.*

(He lunges at **ISADORA**, *who holds her ground.* **YOLOT** *interrupts screaming, clutching her belly. Lights come down except for a ghostly spotlight on* **YOLOT**.*)*

YOLOT. Ah! He's coming! He's coming!

(The wolves outside howl in agitation. **YOLOT***'s labor-pain cries, her arching back, become a howl.)*

(Lights shift.)

Scene Seven

*(Lights up, **YOLOT** is in labor, she's on the bed. **ISADORA** props pillows behind **YOLOT**. **SÉPTIMO** finishes attaching a new chain to the iron collar around **YOLOT**'s neck, once again chaining her to the bed. He attaches the collar's key to the ring that hangs from his belt.)*

*(**ROCÍO** enters and places a bowl of warm water nearby. She begins to lift **YOLOT**'s nightgown over her bent knees, but then stops and looks at **SÉPTIMO**. **ISADORA** notes this.)*

ISADORA. Séptimo, bring in more logs for the fire.

SÉPTIMO. There's more than enough firewood here.

ISADORA. I was asking for you to leave the room.

SÉPTIMO. I'm not about to leave you three alone.

ISADORA. She's not going anywhere. None of us are. You can afford to give us a little privacy.

SÉPTIMO. What? For her modesty? She was sleeping naked in the stable. And you don't have to worry about me, either. I've seen birthings before, Isadora. Saw my father pull a calf out of its mother by the hind legs once.

ISADORA. She's not livestock. Give her at least a little bit of dignity.

SÉPTIMO. No. I want to be here when it's born. I want to hold it in my own two hands.

*(**YOLOT** lets out a long cry. The wolves howl in response. Then the sound of the wolves snarling and a horse squealing in distress. **ROCÍO** goes to the window.)*

ROCÍO. It's the mare!

*(**SÉPTIMO** jumps to the window, pushes **ROCÍO** to one side in order to see what is happening outside.)*

SÉPTIMO. No!

> (**SÉPTIMO** *grabs his rifle and runs outside.)*

> (*Beat.*)

YOLOT. *(To* **ROCÍO**.*)* Did you get it, *vieja*?

> (**ROCÍO** *reveals* **SÉPTIMO***'s keys and hands them to* **ISADORA** *who begins to unlock* **YOLOT***'s collar.* **ROCÍO** *looks out the window.)*

ROCÍO. He's chasing after them.

ISADORA. Into the woods?

ROCÍO. *Sí.*

ISADORA. *(To* **YOLOT**.*)* How's that?

YOLOT. Better.

> (*Gunshots. The women freeze.*)

ISADORA. *(To* **ROCÍO**.*)* Is the mare hurt?

ROCÍO. No, but badly spooked.
I can't see Séptimo.

YOLOT. *(To* **ISADORA**.*)* She's all right. I told them not to wound her.
(To **ROCÍO**.*)* Don't worry, they'll keep Séptimo occupied.

> (*A slight moment as* **ISADORA** *process what* **YOLOT** *just said.)*

ISADORA. You "told" them to attack the mare? ...What are you?

> (**YOLOT** *is silent.)*

YOLOT. *(Eventually.)* I'm like them out there.
They haven't left the property because they're waiting for me to join them.
They are my brothers.

ISADORA. The wolves?

YOLOT. Yes.
I come from that part of the world that exists between shadows. A part of the world unseen by human eyes.
And I must get back there.

I took this form so I could carry what Death has already claimed. That is why I am here, to ferry the departed across the river to the other side.

I came for your son, Isadora.

ISADORA. My son is buried next to the stable.

YOLOT. Yes, his little body is still there, but his spirit...

> (**YOLOT** *caresses her belly.*)

...is inside me.

> (*After a moment,* **ISADORA** *puts her hands on* **YOLOT***'s belly.*)

ISADORA. My son.

> (**ISADORA** *pulls her hand away quickly.*)

He kicked! I thought you said it was his spirit.

YOLOT. It is. But I've stayed here longer than I was meant to. He's something in between spirit and flesh now.

> (*A beat as* **ISADORA** *puts her hands again on* **YOLOT***'s belly.*)

ISADORA. I wish that he could stay. I wish that...

> (**ISADORA** *shakes her head and pulls her hands off* **YOLOT***'s belly.*)

No. He can't stay, can he? Because what would he become with a father like Séptimo?

YOLOT. I'm sorry. I'm not meant for this world. I must return. I must –

> (**YOLOT** *experiences a powerful labor contraction. She falls back into bed.*)

It's too late!

ISADORA. You have plenty of time. Come on.

YOLOT. No, Isadora. It's happening. Your son wants the life he was denied.

> (*Another heavy contraction pain,* **YOLOT** *begins to almost pant.*)

It's no use. I'll be trapped in this body. Trapped on this side of the river.

ISADORA. You can't go back without him?

YOLOT. I cannot return an empty vessel. I must be carrying, I must be **with** spirit. If he's born here I'll have no claim on him. He would have to die again.

ISADORA. You mean kill him?

YOLOT. Yes.

ISADORA. No. No, we can't do that. I can't –

> (*YOLOT cries out again.* ROCÍO *and* ISADORA *help her sit up in bed.* ROCÍO *looks under* YOLOT*'s nightgown.*)

ROCÍO. It's time.
> (*To* YOLOT.) You have to push.

> (ISADORA *sits behind* YOLOT *to help hold/ brace her.*)

YOLOT. (*Tearful.*) I can't.

ISADORA. Yes, you can.

YOLOT. No. You don't understand. This isn't how it happens on the other side. I've never done this before.
It hurts!

ISADORA. I know.

ROCÍO. Push!

> (YOLOT *pushes.*)

ISADORA. Listen to me. What's breaking inside you, it's a miracle. It's a new life. Your new life. As a mother.

ROCÍO. Push!

> (YOLOT *pushes,* ISADORA *supports her.*)

ISADORA. Use the pain. Don't be afraid of it. Let yourself be forged in it. Let it make you stronger. Let yourself be transformed.

ROCÍO. Push!

> (YOLOT *pushes.*)

ISADORA. You will be unleashed. You will be instinct and ferocity. You will find the strength – the will – to shed your past self. You – are – reborn!

ROCÍO. *Lo veo.* One more push.

> (**YOLOT** *delivers one final push,* **ISADORA** *supports her.*)

> (*A moment as* **ROCÍO** *takes the unseen baby from between* **YOLOT**'s *legs.* **ROCÍO** *cleans the baby in her lap. Eventually he lets out one cry.* **YOLOT** *begins to cry.* **ISADORA** *consoles her.*)

ISADORA. You did it.

YOLOT. No, Isadora. This isn't my miracle. It's yours.

> (**YOLOT** *cries.*)

ISADORA. It will be all right. I promise.

YOLOT. How? I can't go home now.

> (*The baby cries.* **ISADORA** *goes to* **ROCÍO**. *A moment – none of the women speak. They all stare at the baby.* **ISADORA** *moves towards the baby, but stops herself.*)

ISADORA. (*To* **YOLOT**.) Is it all right if I...?

YOLOT. He's your son, Isadora.

> (**ROCÍO** *puts the baby in* **ISADORA**'s *arms.*)

ISADORA. My son.

ROCÍO. ...Isadora – *hija,* what are we going to do? You can't let Séptimo have him.

ISADORA. No. I won't let that happen.

> (*Beat.*)

(*To* **YOLOT**.) You said you can only go back if you're carrying a spirit.

YOLOT. Yes.

ISADORA. Any spirit?

> (*A beat as* **YOLOT** *searches* **ISADORA**'s *face.*)

There's a way.

YOLOT. How?

ISADORA. Rocío.

ROCÍO. *Sí, hija.*

ISADORA. Go find a shovel.

(Lights shift.)

Scene Eight

(Lights up. **YOLOT** *stands at the window looking out.* **ROCÍO** *is at the bed swaddling the quiet infant.)*

ROCÍO. When he asked for her hand in marriage the entire household was surprised.

They had barely spoken more than a dozen words to one another. He had been to the house many times, of course. But to see her brothers. And then to buy her father's mare.

His other horse was lamed.

He told everyone that a snake had scared it. That it took off running through a thicket of trees. That the thorns and branches scratched its eyes.

But that was a lie.

I saw him one night, leaving the house. The horse didn't want him to mount. Kept moving away as he tried to get into the saddle.

He hit it across the face with his riding crop. Again and again. Until finally it submitted.

When he asked for her hand, Isadora was beside herself. Happy. Everyone was. And I, I didn't say a thing.

YOLOT. Why not?

ROCÍO. I wanted to be wrong. I wanted to believe he was what he appeared to be: an honorable and good man. But I knew. Deep down inside I knew when I saw him beating his horse. That in that moment he revealed his true nature.

But I kept it to myself. The entire family thought the world of him. To say otherwise would have shattered Isadora's happiness. Would have put her brothers at odds with a man they called their friend.

Even after devoting my entire life to *la familia*, I didn't dare risk upsetting them.

A *criada* should know her place.

What could I do? Would they have believed me? What if they threw me out? I'm too old to be out on my own. That's what I told myself. That they wouldn't believe me. That it wouldn't matter if I was silent. But it was a coward's way of thinking. I knew it then and I know it now.

So I came here. At least by her side I could endure it with her.

> *(Beat.)*

It started slowly.

I would find her crying. Confused. He had said something cruel. He chipped away at her with words. And my beautiful, happy girl withdrew into herself. Perhaps she knew then what was coming.

It took him a month before he actually let his hand fly.

That first time. I told her we could go home. Our real home.

The next morning he was weeping at her feet. Begging for forgiveness. He kissed her bruise so tenderly.

She wanted to believe the lie. So she did.

But by the time she realized the truth she was too far along with child to travel. And she was right, he would never let her go with his son.

> *(**ROCÍO** has finished swaddling the baby.)*

There. All cleaned up and dressed.

> *(**YOLOT** puts a hand on **ROCÍO**'s shoulder. A moment of acknowledgement.)*

> *(**ROCÍO** places a sling around **YOLOT** and puts the baby into it. **ROCÍO** then secures the sling around **YOLOT**'s body with another swath of material.)*

YOLOT. Will you tell her?

ROCÍO. She wouldn't forgive me.

YOLOT. That's the coward thinking again.

ROCÍO. Yes, yes, it is.

Perhaps the only place for penance like that is after death.

YOLOT. Perhaps.

ROCÍO. When it's my time, I hope it is you who comes for me.

YOLOT. I make no promises, *vieja.*
Where's Isadora?

ROCÍO. Waiting.

YOLOT. There won't be much time once he's figured out what she's done.

ROCÍO. She'll be here.

YOLOT. And she won't change her mind?

ROCÍO. She'll keep her promise.

> *(The howl of a wolf – very close.)*

YOLOT. They're ready.

> *(**YOLOT** opens the window and leans out a bit. Unseen by the women, **SÉPTIMO** with his rifle quietly enters through the front door and watches them.)*

Feel that night air. I can't wait to run through it. I'm coming, *hermanos.*

> *(**SÉPTIMO** emerges from the shadows.)*

SÉPTIMO. And where do you think you're going?

YOLOT. Back where I came from.

> *(**SÉPTIMO** advances, **YOLOT** and **ROCÍO** circle around the bed, keeping the bed between them and **SÉPTIMO**.)*

SÉPTIMO. Oh, no you're not. Not with that baby.

YOLOT. You can't have it. It isn't for you.

SÉPTIMO. I believe we had an agreement.

YOLOT. I never agreed.

SÉPTIMO. That's beside the point. I told you I'd let you leave if you left the baby. But if I have to take it from you, woman, then there's no guarantee you'll leave here at all.

YOLOT. You want this child? Come and take it.

> (**SÉPTIMO** *leaps over the bed.* **ROCÍO** *puts herself in his path as* **YOLOT** *bolts for the door.)*

ROCÍO. No!

> (**ROCÍO** *grabs the rifle and won't let go.* **SÉPTIMO** *releases the rifle and throws* **ROCÍO** *out of his way, she lands on the bed.* **YOLOT** *runs out the door,* **SÉPTIMO** *follows.)*

SÉPTIMO. *(Exiting.)* ¡Ven pa'ca, mujer!

> (**ROCÍO** *rushes to the window, leans out to watch. From the other side of the stage enters* **ISADORA** *holding a baby, it cries.* **ISADORA** *quickly crosses the stage to lock the door of the house.)*

ROCÍO. He's coming back.

> *(The wolves howl, they sound as if they've multiplied in number.)*

> *(The door rotates slightly so* **SÉPTIMO** *is visible on one side and* **ISADORA** *on the other.* **SÉPTIMO** *tries to open the door and finds it locked.)*

SÉPTIMO. Unlock the door! Rocío! Isadora!

ISADORA. I'm right here, Séptimo.

SÉPTIMO. Let me in. I need my gun. That bitch has our child.

ISADORA. No, Séptimo. He's right here. With me.
It was a ruse, Séptimo. We dug one up to lure you from this house.

SÉPTIMO. Dug up? ...

ISADORA. That's right. That grave by the stable is empty now.

SÉPTIMO. *¡Jodida!* Open this door! Open it!

ISADORA. No, Séptimo.

(Measured.) Listen to me: you're staying outside.

> *(A series of wolf growls followed by snarling and the snapping of jaws.* **SÉPTIMO** *turns around to face the unseen wolves.)*

SÉPTIMO. Isadora, please! The wolves are coming.

ISADORA. I know.

Listen to me, Séptimo. You died an honorable death. You saw the wolves closing in and you pushed me and our baby inside. You saved us. I will tell everyone just how brave you were. How you faced a pack of ravenous wolves, knowing full well they'd tear you apart.

This is my gift to you, Séptimo – the prestige you so desired in life, you will have in death. I hope you finally find the peace that has eluded you.

SÉPTIMO. No! No! Isadora, open the door. Things will be different. I'll change. I – I'll never strike you again. I promise.

ISADORA. And that's a promise I can help you keep. Goodbye, Séptimo.

> *(Low growl of the wolves, very close.)*

SÉPTIMO. Isadora!

ISADORA!

> *(The door rotates away, hiding* **SÉPTIMO** *behind it. The sound of the wolves attacking* **SÉPTIMO. ISADORA** *moves away from the door.* **ROCÍO** *crosses herself and then spits.)*
>
> *(Lights down. In the dark the sound of the wolves and* **SÉPTIMO**'s *screams die out.)*

Epilogue

(Lights up, a soft halo of light on **ISADORA** *rocking the baby to sleep.* **ROCÍO** *enters and puts a shawl over* **ISADORA***'s shoulders.)*

ROCÍO. Is he hungry?

ISADORA. I already fed him.

*(***ROCÍO*** puts a hand above* **ISADORA***'s breast.)*

ROCÍO. Your milk has come?

ISADORA. Just in time for the baby.

ROCÍO. *Que bueno.*

*(***ROCÍO*** looks out the window.)*

ISADORA. What do you see?

ROCÍO. Just the mare.

There's no sign of them. The wolves…or Séptimo.

ISADORA. They'll be at the river by now.

ROCÍO. I can't wait for *la familia* to arrive. They can't come soon enough.

ISADORA. Think of it, *vieja.* By the end of this month the house will be filled with love and laughter.

ROCÍO. …What will you tell them – when they ask about Séptimo?

ISADORA. The truth. I'll tell them that Séptimo thought he saw a wolf running off with the baby.

I'll tell them that he chased after it, not knowing our child was safe inside.

I'll tell them that all we found the next morning were his shredded boots.

It was a fair trade, *vieja.* Séptimo for the baby.

(To baby.) Your second chance had a high cost, *hijo.* You must take care not to waste it.

(Lights dim on the women until they are almost silhouettes. On the other side of the stage ghostly lights up on **YOLOT** *in the woods.)*

She is naked and pregnant. She experiences a swift kick from the "baby.")

YOLOT. Kick all you want, Séptimo. Soon we'll cross the river and on the other side will be many trials. Difficult trials.

Perhaps the misfortunes you lived through in this life will help you navigate Míctlan.

*(A wolf calls to **YOLOT**.)*

Time to go.

*(Lights down on **YOLOT** as she disappears into the woods. Lights back up on **ISADORA** and **ROCÍO**. **ROCÍO** stands at the window.)*

ISADORA. The nightmare is over now, *vieja*.

ROCÍO. *Sí.* Winter is always followed by Spring.

ISADORA. Yes, it is.

(Beat.)

ROCÍO. Look at that moon. I've never seen it so big and bright.

ISADORA. *(To baby.)* Hear that? It shines for you, *mi'jito*.

*(**ROCÍO** leaves the window to stand over **ISADORA**'s shoulder.)*

ROCÍO. Have you chosen a name for him?

ISADORA. We will call him Benicio. Because he will be a good man.

(Lights down slowly.)

End of Play

NATIONAL NEW PLAY NETWORK

National New Play Network is an alliance of professional theaters that work together in innovative ways to develop, produce, and extend the life of new plays. NNPN's flagship initiative, the Rolling World Premiere (RWP) program, supports three or more Member Theaters that choose to fully mount the same new play within eighteen months, agreeing to share the World Premiere designation amongst them. This allows the playwright to develop their new work with distinct creative teams in multiple communities, making adjustments based on what is learned from each production's artists and audiences.

To date, NNPN has championed the RWPs of more than ninety new plays that have gone on to receive hundreds of subsequent productions across the US and around the world, been nominated for and/or won the Pulitzer Prize, Steinberg/ATCA, Stavis, PEN, and Blackburn awards, and adapted into feature films. The playwrights supported by the RWP program are emerging, established, and renowned artists, many of whom credit an NNPN RWP as a major step in their career. Learn more about NNPN and RWPs at www.nnpn.org.

www.ingramcontent.com/pod-product-compliance
Lightning Source LLC
Chambersburg PA
CBHW070402120726
47909CB00008B/2954